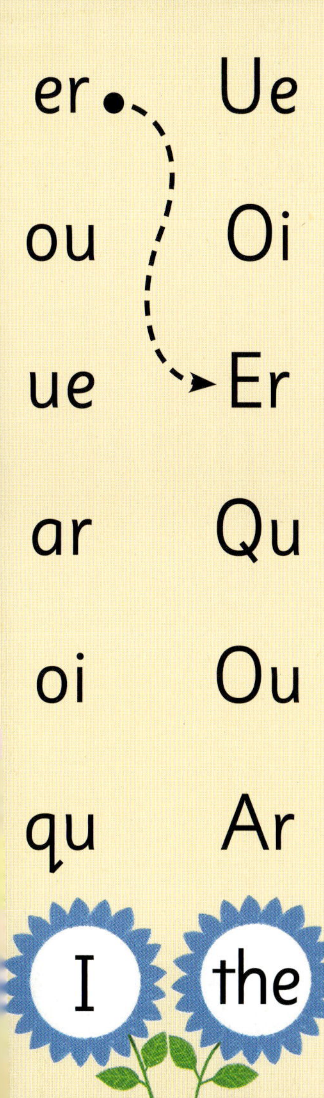

This is Mervin.

This is Mervin's garden.
□ boots
□ a fork
□ soil
□ a squirrel
□ a statue

In his garden, Mervin has carrots, beetroot, radishes, parsnips...

...and slugs and snails.
Munch!
Chomp!

"Get off!" shouts Mervin.

Yuck! Get out!

But Mervin has a cunning plan.
A-ha! I have a cunning plan.

Mervin has a big box and a wooden house.

Quick, Mervin!
It's getting dark.

Munch, crunch!

Chomp, chomp,
sniff!

Next morning,
the slugs and snails have gone!